# Elliot's Park

## Saving Mister Nibbles

### BY PATRICK CARMAN
### ILLUSTRATED BY JIM MADSEN

**Orchard Books**
An Imprint of Scholastic Inc. ✦ New York

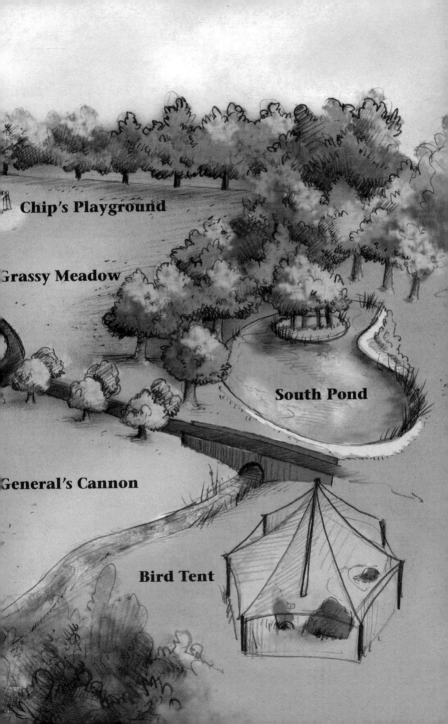

Chip's Playground

Grassy Meadow

South Pond

General's Cannon

Bird Tent

For Reece Carman and Ken Geist,
two people who love Elliot's Park
as much as I do!

Text copyright © 2008 by Patrick Carman. • Illustrations copyright © 2008 by Jim Madsen. • Map illustration © 2008 by Squire Broel. All rights reserved. Published by Orchard Books, an imprint of Scholastic Inc., *Publishers since 1920*. ORCHARD BOOKS and design are registered trademarks of Watts Publishing Group, Ltd., used under license. SCHOLASTIC and associated logos are trademarks and/or registered trademarks of Scholastic Inc. No part of this publication may be reproduced, stored in a retrieval system, or transmitted in any form or by any means, electronic, mechanical, photocopying, recording, or otherwise, without written permission of the publisher. For information regarding permission, write to Orchard Books, Scholastic Inc., Permissions Department, 557 Broadway, New York, NY 10012.

This book was originally published in hardcover in 2008.

ISBN-13: 978-0-545-01941-5 • ISBN-10: 0-545-01941-9

12 11 10 9 8 7 6 5 4 3 2 1          9 10 11 12 13 14/0

Printed in the U.S.A.          40

First Scholastic paperback printing, January 2009.

Book design by Alison Klapthor

# CHAPTERS

# CHAPTER 1

# A Party in Elliot's Park

"**Go long!**" shouted Elliot.

His best friend, Chip, faked right, flipped in the air, and raced out under the trees. Chip was a dangerous sort of squirrel.

"I got it! I got it!" Chip yelled. But he didn't get it.

He ran smack into Elliot's sister, Twitch, instead. The two rolled like a tumbleweed over the grass. When they stopped, the ball bonked Chip on the head.

"Ouch," he said, rubbing his squirrel noggin.

"Come quick! Come quick!" shouted Twitch. "I have something to show you."

"Can't you see we're busy?" asked Chip.

"It can't wait! You have to come right now!"

Twitch was jumping up and down when Elliot arrived.

"Did you drink a soda pop for breakfast?" asked Elliot.

"I did, I did, I did!" answered his sister. She burped. It was a big burp, and it was grape-flavored.

"What's so important that we have to come right now?" asked Elliot, pushing up his large square glasses.

"There's a party at the playground!" answered Twitch. "A birthday party!"

Elliot put one of his paws on Twitch's shoulder.

"People have parties in our park all the

time. You should try to get used to it."

"But this one is different!" shouted Twitch.

She stopped jumping and said, "One of the presents is a squirrel."

Twitch never lied, but a squirrel as a present? That was hard to believe.

"Are you sure?" asked Elliot.

"Come see for yourself!" said Twitch.

Chip's tail shook with excitement as he looked toward the playground.

But Elliot was a safe sort of squirrel.

He was not dangerous like his best friend, Chip.

"We'll send Crash first," said Elliot. "It's the safest way to find out what's really going on."

Chip couldn't wait. He was already racing for the playground.

"Be careful, Chip!" shouted Elliot.

Twitch started running for the BIG tree.
"Come on! We'd better hurry."

When they arrived near the top of the BIG
tree, Elliot opened his tiny door and went
inside.

He came back out with a little silver
bicycle bell and pulled on the lever.

*Ding-ding-ding.*

Off in the distance they could hear
someone coming.

"There, there, there!" shouted Twitch.
She sounded a lot like the bell. "I see her."

A flying squirrel with big goggles and a fancy scarf was getting closer. She made a wobbly approach and crashed into the trunk of the tree. Then she slid down and stood in front of Elliot and Twitch.

"You rang?" said Crash in her British accent.

"There's trouble at the playground," said Elliot. "We need a flyover."

"A mission, you say?" answered Crash. She liked being the only flying squirrel in the park. "Wait for me here. I shall return!"

Up, up, and away she went, flying through the trees.

*Ding-ding-ding.* Twitch had picked up the bell.

She liked to make the ringing sound. *Ding-ding-ding.*

Elliot held out his paw. "Give me the bell," he said.

Twitch handed it over, and Elliot put it back inside the house.

When he came out, he heard something up in the sky.

"There, there, there!" shouted Twitch.

Crash tumbled into Elliot's closed door with a thump. Then she stood straight up.

"Reporting in, sir," she said. "There's a birthday party in full swing."

Twitch bounced up and down with excitement. Her pop–top necklace jingled loudly.

"And is one of the gifts really a squirrel?" asked Elliot.

Crash looked seriously toward the playground.

"It is indeed, sir," she said. "Chip is trying to take it from them."

"What!" cried Elliot. This job was too big even for Chip.

"We need to save that squirrel!" said Elliot.

"Yippee, yippee, yippee!" shouted Twitch. She and Elliot raced down the tree.

Crash flew overhead.

Soon the three of them were at the playground.

And then Elliot saw the party for himself.

This was going to be a very large problem to solve!

# CHAPTER 2

# Hello! My Name Is Mister Nibbles!

**Elliot liked** to get a really good look at a problem before trying to solve it. He looked back and forth at the whole playground. Then he looked back and forth again. Then he looked back and forth five more times.

This is what he saw:

A group of children and parents were sitting in a circle next to the big slide.

They were opening presents. It looked and sounded like a regular birthday party.

There was a lot of wrapping paper. There were bows and a cake.

There were children screaming.

Elliot moved his eyes slowly up the ladder of the big slide. There he saw something that made him nervous.

Chip was perched at the top!

"Chip!" screamed Elliot. "Come down from there!"

Chip turned around fast and lost his balance. He slid down the slide with alarming speed. At the bottom he shot into the air and then landed in the wood chips.

*Phwooooop!* Chip rolled head over heels
about seven times before he stopped.
All the children laughed.

"Over here!" cried Elliot.

Chip darted across the playground.
He zoomed up the side of the tree to join
the group.

"That parent!" He pointed at a redheaded lady with lots of freckles. "Has given that child!" He pointed to a child with red hair and lots of freckles. "A SQUIRREL!"

"Are you sure about this?" asked Elliot. He tapped his little squirrel foot on the tree branch. He crossed his arms over his chest. "I don't believe you."

Chip opened his mouth to reply. One of his two front teeth had a missing corner. Elliot and Twitch both thought it looked dangerous.

"Follow me," said Chip. "I'll show you!"

Chip darted down the tree and zipped across the playground. He waved his paw for everyone to follow.

"Tallyho!" said Crash, jumping from the tree. She flew in fast between the swings and the horseshoe pit.

When she landed, there was a lot of noise and flying wood chips.

All the kids and parents gazed in amazement.

While everyone was busy looking at Crash, Elliot and Twitch raced down the tree. They joined Chip at the top of the jungle gym. When they were all looking down on the party, Chip pointed his little squirrel finger.

"There!" he shouted.

A silly-looking squirrel was lying on its side with all the other gifts. It wasn't moving.

"Why doesn't he run away?" cried Elliot.

"Maybe they stepped on him. Maybe he's injured! I don't know!" said Chip.

Just then the boy with the red hair and all the freckles picked up the squirrel.

"Run away! Run away!" yelled Twitch. But the odd squirrel didn't move.

"That child must have a grip of steel," said Chip.

Then — to everyone's surprise — the squirrel began to speak.

The boy was pressing the squirrel's ear. He was making it speak!

*"Hello! My name is Mister Nibbles. What is your name?"*

It was a squeaky voice.

The children all laughed at Mister Nibbles, so the boy pressed the ear again.

*"You are my best friend!"* said Mister Nibbles.

"Run, Mister Nibbles, run!" said Twitch.

"Fly away if you can!" shouted Crash.

But Mister Nibbles just sat there.

Chip was right. This was an outrage! Elliot had to make a plan to rescue Mister Nibbles.

"Come on!" said Elliot.

Soon the four squirrels were high in the tree, looking down on the party.

The children and parents were about to leave.

Elliot looked at Crash.

"Can you fly over and follow Mister Nibbles? We need to know where they take him."

All the squirrels thought this was a good idea.

"Brilliant!" said Crash.

The boy with the red hair and freckles took one last zoom down the slide. He picked up Mister Nibbles.

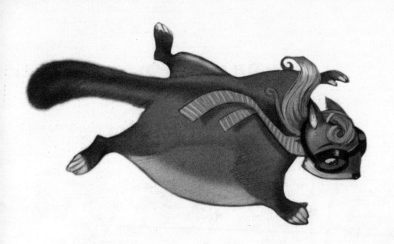

"Can we return this?" he asked his mother.

"What does that mean?" asked Elliot from the tree.

"I don't know. But it can't be good!" said Chip.

Mister Nibbles was put into a box with the other gifts. Soon everyone was gone.

It was quiet in the park.

Thank goodness Crash was flying overhead. She was dodging parked cars and power lines, keeping a close eye on Mister Nibbles.

# CHAPTER 3

# Scratchy Spurs

**Elliot was sitting** in his favorite chair, thinking very hard.

He had returned to his home in the BIG tree and closed the door.

Twitch and Chip stood outside waiting for Crash to return.

When he thought really, really hard, Elliot

tapped his foot. The harder he thought,
the faster he tapped. Saving Mister Nibbles
was a real whopper, so his foot kept tapping
faster.

A picture fell down.

A nut rolled off a shelf.

Things were falling everywhere! His foot
tapped faster and faster and faster!

Then Elliot fell out of his chair.

He picked up all the things that had fallen
and pushed his glasses back up on his nose.
He straightened his tie and sat back down.

Just then, there was a loud knock at the
door.

"I'm never going to solve this problem,"
Elliot said.

When he opened his door, Elliot found
that Crash had returned.

"I have word," said Crash. She shook her

tail free of twigs and leaves. "Shall I come inside?"

"There isn't room for all of us inside," said Elliot. "I think here on the limb will be perfect."

Crash removed her goggles. There was a grim look on her face.

"The boy has taken Mister Nibbles to the yellow house," she said. "I believe you know the house with the two dogs."

"Good work!" said Chip. "The yellow house is just across the street from the park."

"Brilliant!" Crash said. "Just brilliant!"

Elliot needed to figure out how to save Mister Nibbles. He started to go back inside his tree, but then he changed his mind.

"I'm going for a walk," he said. He was having a hard time thinking with so much noise. What he really needed was advice, and he knew just where to get it.

Elliot told his friends to meet him just before dark. He also told them to bring three other squirrels — Sparkle, Stitches, and Pistachio.

Elliot zipped and zoomed up and down trees on his way through the park. Along the way he saw Roscoe and Coconut loose in the park.

Roscoe and Coconut were giant, squirrel-chasing dogs. They lived in the backyard of the yellow house. One was black, and one was white. Both needed baths. Roscoe and Coconut loved to chase Elliot and all of his friends.

"I'd better be careful," said Elliot.

He kept zipping and zooming up and down the trees. He stayed far away from Roscoe and Coconut.

Finally, Elliot reached the edge of the big pond in the park. He looked out over the water and saw Wilma.

Wilma was the largest white goose anyone had ever seen.

Elliot's fur shook.

Wilma hated squirrels.

Elliot snuck carefully around the side of the pond until he came to an old fir tree. The tree looked like it was about to fall over. He raced up and found Scratchy Spurs on the same limb he was always on.

Scratchy Spurs was asleep. He had a little cowboy hat on.

There was a piece of grass from the lawn

in the park hanging out of his mouth. Funny little spurs were stuck to his feet. There was a twig lying across his lap — his cane — and it shook as Scratchy Spurs snored.

"Scratchy?" said Elliot.

He would need to say it louder. Scratchy Spurs couldn't hear all that well.

"Scratchy!" he yelled.

Scratchy Spurs didn't wake up. He started scratching at the itchy fur under his chin.

Scratchy Spurs scratched a lot. It was one of the reasons everyone called him Scratchy Spurs.

Elliot took the cane off the old squirrel's lap and bonked him on the knee with it.

That did the trick.

Scratchy Spurs was awake. The first thing he did was scratch his belly. Then he scratched his nose. Then he took off his cowboy hat and scratched the top of his head. His spurs jangled when he scratched. This made Wilma honk loudly from the pond.

"I reckon that's my cane," Scratchy Spurs said to Elliot.

"Here you are," said Elliot. He handed the cane back.

"What brings you to my neck of the woods?"

Elliot told Scratchy Spurs all about Mister Nibbles.

For a moment, Scratchy Spurs didn't say anything.

Elliot thought maybe he'd fallen asleep again.

But then Scratchy Spurs started talking. He could see that Elliot was in a little bit of a hurry.

"What you need to do is get in that house," said Scratchy Spurs. "But I think you'll have more luck at night."

And then Scratchy Spurs gave Elliot a whole bunch of good ideas. Pretty soon, *BAM!* The problem was solved in Elliot's head!

"Thanks, Scratchy!" howled Elliot, racing down the tree. "You're the best!"

"Don't you worry," said Scratchy Spurs. "I'm always watching out for you."

Scratchy Spurs didn't get up. He scratched

a little. He gazed down in the pond at Wilma, who had moved closer and was staring up at him.

"Howdy, chicken!" he hollered.

Wilma hated being called a chicken. She began squawking loudly, flapping her wings on the water. Elliot made his way back home through the park.

## CHAPTER 4

# Into the Yellow House

**Elliot held** a little clipboard in one paw and a pencil in the other. It was night in the park and he was busy checking to see if everyone had arrived.

"Chip!"

"Here!"

Elliot checked Chip's name off on the list and handed him a flashlight. Trying to get inside the yellow house to free Mister Nibbles was going to be scary and it would be dark. Flashlights were a must.

"Sparkle!"

"Here!"

Elliot checked off Sparkle's name and held out a flashlight.

"No need," she said. "I'm a stargazer!"

Sparkle had shiny, star-shaped earrings to prove it. There were dangers at night and she knew best how to keep everyone away from them.

The biggest of these were the three owls that lived in the park. The owls liked to chase squirrels that came out in the night, and Sparkle could hide from them.

"Stitches!"

"Here!"

Stitches was the park doctor. She wore a spiffy white coat.

Elliot wanted her close by in case Mister Nibbles needed medical attention.

"Pistachio!"

There was no reply, so Elliot looked up from his clipboard. Pistachio was trying very hard to break into a walnut.

"Pistachio!"

The young squirrel looked up with the walnut still unopened. It was lodged between his teeth.

"Put the nut down, Pistachio," said Elliot.

Pistachio ignored him, so Elliot had to get stern.

"Put down the nut!"

Pistachio dropped the walnut and sat down on top of it.

"Here!" he said.

Only two more names to call, thought Elliot.

"Twitch!"

"Here!" *Hiccup*.

Twitch was jumpy and she said "here" very loudly. She also had the hiccups.

"Are you sure you want to come along?" asked Elliot, holding out a flashlight.

"I'll be — *hiccup* — just fine. Don't you — *hiccup* — worry about a thing!"

Crash was the only other squirrel in the group. She bumped into a lot of things when she flew during the day. But at night it was downright scary to let her fly.

"Crash!"

"Present," said Crash.

"We're going to strap this to your back," said Elliot.

He had a flashlight in his hand and he turned it on.

Crash was pleased with the idea.

"Let's get cracking!" she said.

Chip pulled a piece of string from the bushes. Soon an army of little squirrel paws had strapped the flashlight on tight.

Elliot looked over his notes. He gazed into the darkness of the park.

And then he set his plan into action.

"Operation Saving Mister Nibbles begins."

Elliot checked his watch.

"Now!"

Sparkle was the first to go. All the other squirrels turned on their flashlights and followed. Tiny beams of light danced at their feet.

Sparkle stopped about every ten seconds to gaze at the stars. She liked pointing out the big ones. Elliot wondered if they would ever reach the yellow house.

"Sparkle," he said, "we're running out of time. Please, let's stick to the plan."

Sparkle followed a twisty-turny path to avoid the owls.

Crash flew between the trees overhead.

Finally, all the squirrels arrived at the edge of the park.

The time had come to cross the street.

Crash ran the flashlight back and forth along the road. Everyone looked both ways. And then, all at once, Elliot and his friends ran for the other side.

Crash flew over the street and landed on the roof of the yellow house. From there, she saw two big dogs in the backyard.

"I must report this finding!" said Crash, running across the roof.

When she was at the front of the house, Crash pointed her flashlight down at Elliot. The light was in Elliot's eyes. He held his paws up in front of his face.

"Don't go 'round back,"

said Crash. "Roscoe and Coconut are out."

"Those dogs are trouble!" said Elliot. "We'll have to use Plan B to get inside."

He gazed up at Crash.

"Wait for us up there."

The flashlight was really bright in Elliot's eyes.

"And turn that thing off until we come out."

Crash spun in circles trying to turn the flashlight off, but she couldn't reach it. Everyone watched as she lost her balance and tumbled down the roof. She was stuckin the gutter, but the flashlight was turned off.

"Brilliant!" she cried.

Elliot made a check mark on his list of things to do.

Getting safely out of the park, check!

He looked at Twitch and Stitches.

"Tell everyone to switch to Plan B," Elliot said.

"Wait here until the time we planned, then spring into action. Everyone else, TO THE ROOF!"

Each squirrel chose a different way to the top of the yellow house.

Sparkle went up the drainpipe and made the most noise.

Chip darted up a telephone pole and across a power line.

It was the most dangerous way he could find.

Elliot scampered up the wooden fence and dove into the gutter.

Pistachio ran up a tree and onto a limb that hung over the roof.

Elliot made another check mark.

Meet on the roof of the yellow house,
by the front door, check!

"Get into position," said Elliot.

He was looking at Chip, the strongest
of the four squirrels. Chip got inside the
gutter. He let his tail hang free over the
edge of the roof.

"Ready?" asked Elliot.

"Ready," answered Chip.

Pistachio climbed down Chip's tail and
hung on with his claws.

Sparkle followed, holding on to Pistachio's
tail.

"Ouch!" cried Pistachio. "Don't hold on
so tight!"

Elliot climbed down last. He held on
to Sparkle's tail.

There was a sound from inside
the house.

Everyone
froze, hanging
like a long rope
in front of the door.
The noise went away,
and Elliot burst into action.

"Start swinging!" he squeaked.

And they did. Elliot swung out
toward the front yard. He swung
in toward the door. Out toward
the front yard.

"You can do it, Elliot!" cried
Twitch. She and Stitches were
sitting on the white picket fence,
watching the show.

When Elliot came close to
the door again, he reached out
his wee little paw as far as
he could.

*DING–DONG!* He hit the doorbell.

After that, everything moved very fast. Elliot dropped to the ground. Pistachio, Sparkle, and Chip followed. The door opened, and Elliot and his friends were hidden in the bushes next to the door. It was the lady with the red hair and freckles from the party.

The mother of the boy was at the door.

Stitches and Twitch sprang into action! They began squeaking their heads off. Then they stood up on two legs and started dancing.

"Come see these squirrels!" the woman shouted into the house. "They're dancing!"

Soon the dad and the boy were outside with the mom. They crept toward Stitches and Twitch to get a closer look.

Elliot, Sparkle, Pistachio, and Chip all

zipped in through the door.

"We did it! We're inside the yellow house!" said Sparkle.

"Mister Nibbles! We have come to save you!" cried Pistachio.

Elliot and Chip ran up and down the hallway, yelling.

"Mister Nibbles, where are you?"

Sparkle zipped and zoomed along the carpet. Then she hit the slick floor in the kitchen. *Whoooosh!* She tumbled and rolled, crashing into the dishwasher.

Pistachio's eyes were glued to the television.

"Everyone up the stairs!" cried Elliot. "He's not down here!"

When Elliot, Chip, Pistachio, and Sparkle were safely upstairs, Elliot heard the front door close.

The mom, the dad, and the boy had come back inside. They sat down and watched the television.

Elliot hadn't thought it would take so long to find Mister Nibbles. He hadn't planned for this.

They were trapped inside the yellow house!

# CHAPTER 5

# Saving Mister Nibbles!

"**Come out,** Mister Nibbles!" said Elliot.

The four friends searched in the bathroom.

No Mister Nibbles.

They searched the big bedroom.

Still no Mister Nibbles.

Then they came to a room at the very end

of the hall.

"This is the last room in the yellow house," said Chip.

"Mister Nibbles has to be in there," said Pistachio.

Elliot looked at his three companions. They were trapped in the yellow house and he didn't have a plan to get out. He would have to think on his feet!

"Pistachio?"

The young squirrel looked at Elliot.

"You stay at the end of the hall. Keep an eye on them as they watch television."

Pistachio thought this sounded perfect. He liked the television almost as much as he liked nuts. He started running down the hall.

"Hold on!" said Elliot. "I'm not finished yet!"

Pistachio came back as fast as he could and

looked nervously at Elliot.

"If any of them act like they might come up the stairs, warn us so we can hide. Got it?"

"I got it!" said Pistachio.

Elliot saw Sparkle standing in front of the last doorway in the yellow house. She was pointing her flashlight into the darkness. She looked scared.

"What is it?" asked Elliot. "What do you see?"

She wouldn't answer. Chip and Elliot ran to her side and looked up into the beam of light. There were a lot of shadows in the room.

At the top of the bed, hanging off the edge, was a fluffy tail.

"I think it's a cat," whispered Sparkle.

"That's no cat," howled Chip. "It's him!"

"Come down from there, Mister Nibbles!" cried Chip. "We're here to rescue you!"

Mister Nibbles did not move.

"I'm going up there," said Chip. "He must be chained to the bed."

Chip dropped his flashlight. He bolted into the room. He jumped for the blanket covering the bed! Soon he had clawed his way over the edge and out of sight.

Elliot and Sparkle stood in the doorway. It was silent for a long time.

"What's going on up there?" squeaked Elliot.

A quiet little voice came from the top of the bed.

"Guys," said Chip. "We've got a problem up here."

Elliot and Sparkle charged into the room and climbed up the side of the bed.

"That's not Mister Nibbles!" yelled Sparkle.

The tail hanging over the bed belonged to a big, furry, scary-looking dog. It was staring at Chip as though it was going to eat him.

"There are four of us and one of you," said Chip, pointing his little paw at the dog. "Tell us where to find Mister Nibbles and we won't get rough with you."

Elliot thought Chip was crazy, but the dog just sat there! It didn't move or bark. It was weird how it sat so still.

Elliot pointed his flashlight around the bed. He saw a furry-looking monkey and an even furrier-looking duck. Then he pointed his flashlight down on the floor in the corner of the room.

"Mister Nibbles!" he shouted. There, all by himself, sat the squirrel from the park.

Chip whirled around and saw Mister Nibbles. He turned to Sparkle.

"Keep an eye on him," he said, pointing to the dog. Chip and Elliot ran across the bed. They went past the furry-looking monkey and

the even furrier-looking duck. They zoomed
down to the floor and stood in front of
Mister Nibbles.

"We've come to take you back to the park
where you belong!" said Chip. He grabbed
him by the ear and started hauling him
across the floor.

Mister Nibbles shouted,

Boy, Mister Nibbles sure was loud!

"I'm Chip," said Chip. "We have to get you out of here!"

"We better go back and get Sparkle first," said Elliot.

Chip grabbed Mister Nibbles around the middle. He hauled him up the side of the bed.

Elliot followed. When they reached the top, Chip took Mister Nibbles by the ear and flipped him over the edge.

*"You are my best friend!"* Mister Nibbles said.

Chip looked at Elliot.

"Is he talking to you or me?"

"I'm pretty sure he's talking to me," said Elliot.

This bothered Chip. He pushed Mister Nibbles off the side of the bed. When Mister Nibbles hit the floor, he flopped on his side, and said four words: *"I need a hug."*

"Sorry, Mister Nibbles!" said Chip. But Mister Nibbles wouldn't answer.

All three squirrels jumped off the bed and started for the door. Chip carried Mister Nibbles. When they got to the end of the long hallway, Pistachio was gone.

"Where did he go?" asked Sparkle.

Pistachio had left his post at the top of the stairs.

"Oh, no," said Elliot. The three squirrels looked toward the kitchen.

Pistachio was sitting on the dining room table. He had found a bowl of the one kind of nut he loved more than any other. Pistachios!

"I don't see how things could get any worse," said Sparkle.

Then the television shut off.

"I think things just got worse!" said Chip.

The mom and the dad were heading for

the kitchen. They were about to find Pistachio having dinner on their dining room table.

The boy was starting up the stairs.

The plan had failed! They were all in BIG trouble!

And then, just when all seemed lost, Roscoe and Coconut started barking in the backyard. And they didn't just bark. They *BARKED*! They barked so loud the whole family raced for the back door.

"This is our chance!" cried Elliot.

He tore down the stairs faster than he'd ever run before. Sparkle and Chip followed with Mister Nibbles. They zipped and zoomed past the kitchen and found Pistachio.

"Stop eating nuts and run for your life!" screamed Elliot.

All the squirrels arrived at the open back door together. Down the steps they went, hiding in the bushes with Mister Nibbles.

When they peered through the leaves, no one could believe what they saw.

Scratchy Spurs was riding Roscoe like he was a wild bull at the rodeo!

"Cracking good time!" said Crash from the roof. She kept her flashlight aimed right on Scratchy Spurs.

Roscoe and Coconut were both going bananas! But old Scratchy Spurs wouldn't let go. BOY, he really knew how to ride! The mom had a broom in her hands. She was trying to whack old Scratchy Spurs right off the dog! But Roscoe was jumping and running so fast, the mom kept missing.

Elliot raced out in the open and waved.

"We're out of the yellow house! We're out of the yellow house!"

For a moment everyone in the yard stopped, dead silent, and watched. Scratchy Spurs looked back and winked at Elliot.

Scratchy Spurs had Roscoe by the collar. He guided the dog like a true master of the rodeo. Soon he had Roscoe under the one big tree in the backyard. He leaped for the trunk and held on tight. Then the old cowboy slowly made his way up into the tree and out of sight.

# CHAPTER 6

# Elliot's New Roommate

**Mister Nibbles** didn't quite fit in with the other squirrels in the park. But Elliot liked him. Mister Nibbles was a very good listener. He didn't eat a lot. And he never made any messes or knocked anything over.

So Elliot let Mister Nibbles stay with him in his tree house.

Every morning Chip came for a visit. Sometimes when Elliot and Chip felt like laughing they took turns pinching Mister Nibbles on the ear. This always made him talk about silly things, ask for hugs, and forget that they already knew his name. Chip and Elliot thought Mister Nibbles was hilarious.

For Elliot, solving problems was a lot more fun after saving Mister Nibbles. No matter how big the problem was, he knew he and his friends could work together to figure it out.

Elliot heard a *whoosh!* from outside his door, and the squeaky voice of Chip shouting, "I got it! I got it!"

"I sure do love my park," said Elliot.

He got up to leave, squeezing Mister Nibbles' ear as he walked by.

*"You are my best friend!"* said Mister Nibbles.

Elliot smiled. He pushed his glasses up on his nose and straightened his tie. Then he zoomed out the door into the park to play with his friends.

# CAST OF

## Chip

Chip is a bit bigger than other squirrels and

he loves all kinds of sports. He has a history of major accidents, including the time he chipped one of his two large front teeth on the monkey bar. Chip is a daredevil and will try anything. *Distinguishing features: two large front teeth, one chipped; Elliot's best friend.*

## Crash

Crash is the only flying squirrel in Elliot's Park. She has trouble with her landing skills. She

says she is only stopping by on a planned flight around the world. But she always has a good reason for staying. Crash loves to tell about all the places she's been. *Distinguishing features: the only flying squirrel of the bunch; British accent, flying goggles, and often has trouble landing.*

## Daisy, Autumn, and Lefty

All three are young, resourceful, and highly competitive scouts. They are always performing tasks to earn Canyon Squirrel Scout merit badges. *Distinguishing features: bright blue merit badge vests.*

## Elliot

Elliot is a very smart squirrel who lives inside

the largest tree in the park. Whenever a problem arises, Elliot solves it, with the help of his friends. A lovable nerd. *Distinguishing features: big black glasses; he usually wears a collared shirt with a wide tie.*

65

## Mister Nibbles

Mister Nibbles is not an ordinary squirrel; he's

a stuffed animal squirrel. When you press his ear he says five different things. All the other squirrels in the park think Mister Nibbles is hilarious. *Distinguishing features: stuffed; he does not move and says only five things.*

## Pistachio

Pistachio is a nut lover. He will forcibly take

nuts from anyone who enters the park eating them. He is often seen being chased up a tree by parents and dogs. *Distinguishing features: always eating, hiding, or trying to open a nut of one kind or another.*

## Ranger Canyon

Canyon is the Park Ranger squirrel, also a Squirrel Scout leader. He gives out merit badges to Squirrel Scouts for completing park assignments. *Distinguishing features: a Park Ranger tie and a handlebar mustache.*

## Roscoe and Coconut

Roscoe and Coconut are two giant dogs that live across the street from Elliot's Park in the  yellow house. They love to escape from the yard and run into the park to chase the squirrels. Roscoe and Coconut also love to bark. *Distinguishing features: Roscoe is jet-black, Coconut is all white; neither has had a bath in a very long time.*

## Scratchy Spurs

Scratchy Spurs is a retired rodeo squirrel who

dreams of riding one last time. He is the oldest and wisest squirrel in Elliot's Park. Scratchy Spurs and Elliot are buddies. Scratchy Spurs scratches himself a lot. *Distinguishing features: spurs, battered cowboy hat, grass in mouth, twig cane; he speaks with a southern accent.*


## Sparkle

Sparkle loves stars and stargazing. She likes to

be out at night. Sparkle is always getting in trouble with the owls. She likes to sleep in late and sometimes misses breakfast and lunch. *Distinguishing feature: star-shaped earrings.*

## Stitches

Stitches is the park doctor. She is especially well liked by everyone. *Distinguishing features: white coat and a stethoscope around her neck.*

## Twitch

Twitch is Elliot's sister. She loves any type of  sugar, especially soda pop of any flavor. She is very good at finding soda pop. She is hyper almost all of the time. *Distinguishing features: jangling soda pop-top necklace; runs around a lot and is very good at burping.*

## Wilma

Wilma is the biggest goose on the pond in  Elliot's Park. She does not like anyone, especially squirrels. *Distinguishing features: big, white, and loves to honk.*

# Elliot and Chip's Trail Mix

Elliot, Chip, and all their friends from Elliot's
Park love trail mix! There are lots of ingredients the
squirrels like to put in trail mix:

| | |
|---|---|
| Mini pretzels | Peanuts |
| Dried fruit pieces | Mixed nuts |
| Cereal | Banana chips |
| Raisins | Sunflower seeds |
| Chocolate chips | Granola |

You can make your own Trail Mix, just like Elliot
and Chip!

**What you'll need to make this yummy snack:**

- 3 to 5 of your favorite ingredients
- Large sealable plastic bag
- Small sealable plastic bags

Elliot and Chip follow simple steps to create their
Trail Mix. Here's what you do:

# Directions:

1. Pick your favorite ingredients. 3 to 5 is usually just right!

2. Take a handful or two of each ingredient and put them in the large plastic bag.

3. Seal the bag and shake, shake, shake! Mix all the ingredients together!

4. Divide up your trail mix into the small plastic bags.

5. Now you can grab some of Elliot and Chip's Trail Mix whenever you want!

---

## Elliot and Chip know a lot about trail mix!

Here's what they know:

• The snack is sometimes called GORP, which stands for Good Old Raisins and Peanuts.

• People and squirrels all over the world love trail mix, especially as a snack during outdoor activities like hiking and camping.

• In New Zealand and Australia, it is called Scroggin.

• In German-speaking countries, it is called *Studentenfutter*.

• Trail mix is a great snack to bring out on the trails because it is easy to carry, healthy, and gives you lots of energy!

# Create Your Own
# Elliot's Park Adventure

### STEP 1

Sit in a park with your parents or friends and look for some squirrels. Bring along some pencils and a piece of paper.

### STEP 2

Pick one or two squirrels and observe them closely.

Which tree do you think they live in?

What are their favorite foods?

Do they have family and friends?

### STEP 3

Sketch a picture of your squirrels.

Do they have any special features that make them unique?

## STEP 4

Pick names for your squirrels and write them down on your piece of paper.

## STEP 5

Start creating a story about your squirrels.

Take turns adding to the story with a parent or friend, line by line.

See where your adventure takes you.

Tell us your story ideas!

**www.elliotspark.com**

# Sparkle's Starry Night

Create Your Own Tree Constellation!

### Supplies:

- Black Construction Paper
- Pencil or Dark-colored Chalk
- Sharp Pencil or Nail

**1.** Draw a picture of your favorite tree. You can pick one from your backyard, from your favorite park, or even one that you made up.

**2.** Poke small holes along the outline of your drawing. It is best if you poke more than four holes, but fewer than ten. Remember to poke holes in the roots, trunk, leaves, and branches.

**3.** Invent a nutty name for your tree constellation.

**4.** Now hold the construction paper up to a bright light, or tape it to a window. The holes in your drawing will look like bright stars as the light shines through. You have created your very own tree constellation!

**Join Elliot and his friends for a frightful ghost adventure in a teaser chapter from book two, *Haunted Hike*!**

# About the Author
## Patrick Carman

Patrick Carman created the world of Elliot's Park while playing with his daughter in their favorite park. When Patrick is not inventing more squirrel adventures for Elliot and his friends, you can find him at home in Walla Walla, Washington. He is also the author of the bestselling Land of Elyon series.

Patrick Carman and Reece Carman in their favorite park.
Photo courtesy of Reece's older sister, Sierra.
photo © 2008 Sierra Carman